This book belongs to:

_____

To my 5th grade teacher Mr. Boede,
who pushed me not only to try,
but also to think.
—O.C.

For mum and dad.
—C.C.

immedium
inspiring a world of imagination

Immedium, Inc.
P.O. Box 31846
San Francisco, CA 94131
www.immedium.com

First hardcover edition published 2013.

Edited by Eric Searleman
Book design by Stefanie Liang

Printed in Malaysia
10 9 8 7 6 5 4 3 2 1

Library of Congress Cataloging-in-Publication Data

Chin, Oliver Clyde, 1969-
  Julie black belt : the belt of fire / by Oliver Chin ; illustrated by Charlene Chua. -- First hardcover edition.
    pages cm
  Summary: "Julie trains to earn her next Kung Fu belt, but learns valuable lessons from her teacher's master
and a fellow student along her journey"-- Provided by publisher.
  ISBN 978-1-59702-079-4 (hardcover) -- ISBN 1-59702-079-6 (hardcover)
  [1. Kung fu--Fiction. 2. Competition (Psychology)--Fiction. 3. Conduct of life--Fiction.] I. Chua, Charlene, il-
lustrator. II. Title. III. Title: Belt of fire.
  PZ7.C44235Jtm 2013
  [E]--dc23
                    2013001010

ISBN: 978-1-59702-079-4

Julie BLACK BELT

THE BELT OF FIRE

Written by Oliver Chin • Illustrated by Charlene Chua

immedium • San Francisco, CA

Crash! The Jade Crane soared into action. Like a whirlwind, she scattered her opponents like leaves.

Dazed, the bandits stumbled out of the ancient temple. "Ah-ha! The Belt of Fire is finally mine!" she declared.

"Not so fast!"

She spun and saw a strange warrior behind her.

"Whoever wears this belt can become the next Master," warned White Dragon. "Hand it over, or else."

The startled heroine wondered what to do...

Zap! "Julie, finish watching that movie later!" ordered her mother.

"Yeah, it's time for your kung fu class," added Dad.

THE BELT OF FIRE

▶ PLAY MOVIE
SUBTITLES
EXTRAS

"Aw, this is the best part," whined Johnny.

His big sister reminded him, "Don't worry— Brandy Wu always finds a way!"

Quickly, Julie ran to her room to get dressed. Twice a week she practiced martial arts after school.

Julie proudly tied on her new yellow belt. It looked much better than the white one she started with.

After passing her first test, Julie liked kung fu more than ever. She enrolled because she admired the actress Brandy Wu.

SCHOOL OF MARTIAL ARTS

But soon Julie developed her own skill. Now even Johnny wanted to earn a belt!

At school, Dad took a seat as Julie and Johnny greeted their friends. Mr. Fong was their teacher "Sifu".

He called everyone to line up and Julie was ready to go. But the doorbell rang and she turned around.

"Oh, sorry I'm late," a boy apologized. He wore a different uniform but the same color belt as Julie's.

Sifu waved and introduced him, "This is Brandon. His family just moved into the neighborhood, so please welcome him."

"Julie, can you scoot over?" asked Sifu. Brandon bowed, saluted, and went to the head of the class.

Julie was surprised but she whispered to her pal Chloe, "Let's show him a thing or two."

The girls chuckled. However, Sifu got their attention when he stated, "Ok, it's time to warm up."

Quickly the Tiny Tigers began their routine of stretching, jumping jacks, and running laps around the room.

But while Sifu corrected Julie's posture, he praised his new student's punches.

Brandon's loud shouts matched his crisp blocks against Sifu's arm pads.

When the hour was up, Julie's father noted, "That boy has talent."

Back at home, Mom asked, "How was kung fu, Tiger?"

"A new kid started today," gushed Johnny. "He's way better than Julie!"

"No, he's not!" snapped Julie. To avoid worrying about it, she turned the Brandy Wu movie back on.

At the next class Julie vowed to do better, but felt like everyone was watching her.

Brandon was nervous too. He wanted to prove himself and make new friends. Both found their movements didn't flow easily.

Sifu counted, "1, 2, 3," but noticed that Julie's steps and Brandon's forms were cautious.

Julie sensed her head and her heart were in different places. She felt odd as the fun ticked away with each passing minute.

Sifu's clap woke Julie up. "I have special news," he announced. "When I was your age, my teacher was Master Zhou. Next week *my* Sifu is coming to visit us. So help me make a good impression!"

TINY TIGERS

Julie thought, "Sifu has never mentioned him before." Sifu marked his calendar and the students tidied the school. Julie imagined what extraordinary skill, knowledge, and character his Master must possess.

Soon came the day of Master Zhou's arrival. Parents and children waited eagerly. Finally Sifu entered, holding his teacher's arm. "Oh, boy!" thought Julie.

The class greeted her respectfully, "Good afternoon!"

"Hello!" Master Zhou smiled.
"But don't mind me,
I'm here to watch."

"I'm borrowing one of her lessons to help you prepare for your next belt test," Sifu explained. "Once she assigned me a training partner."

"It was hard at first," admitted Sifu, "But she said, 'Though sparks may fly, two blades can sharpen each other.' "

A murmur rippled through the air as Sifu handed out slips of paper. "Ok, see who your partner is!"

As matches were made, one couple got off on the wrong foot. "Ow!" cried Brandon, as Julie banged his elbow.

"Watch out!" yelled Julie as Brandon tripped over her leg.

After observing a few awkward sessions, Master Zhou approached the pair. "Sifu thinks you two need a change of scenery," she suggested. "Tomorrow let's meet outside at the park to practice."

The next day, both kids wanted to show who was better. But Master Zhou advised, "Look before you leap. Watch me first."

She glided from one pose to another. She was calm, confident, and carefree. Everything they were not.

"How did you get so good?" gushed Julie.

Master Zhou smiled. "Kung fu means strengthening your own discipline and ability. Concentrate on improving yourself, and not on impressing others."

The following lessons went smoother. "If you have a clear mind," reflected Master Zhou, "then you can have clear movement."

Soon their energy returned.

Brandon struck like a lion.

Julie soared like an eagle.

In their last week of training, they exercised like a team.

"You remind me of my two favorite students, talented but very competitive," recalled Master Zhou. "Luckily, rivals can learn how to work together."

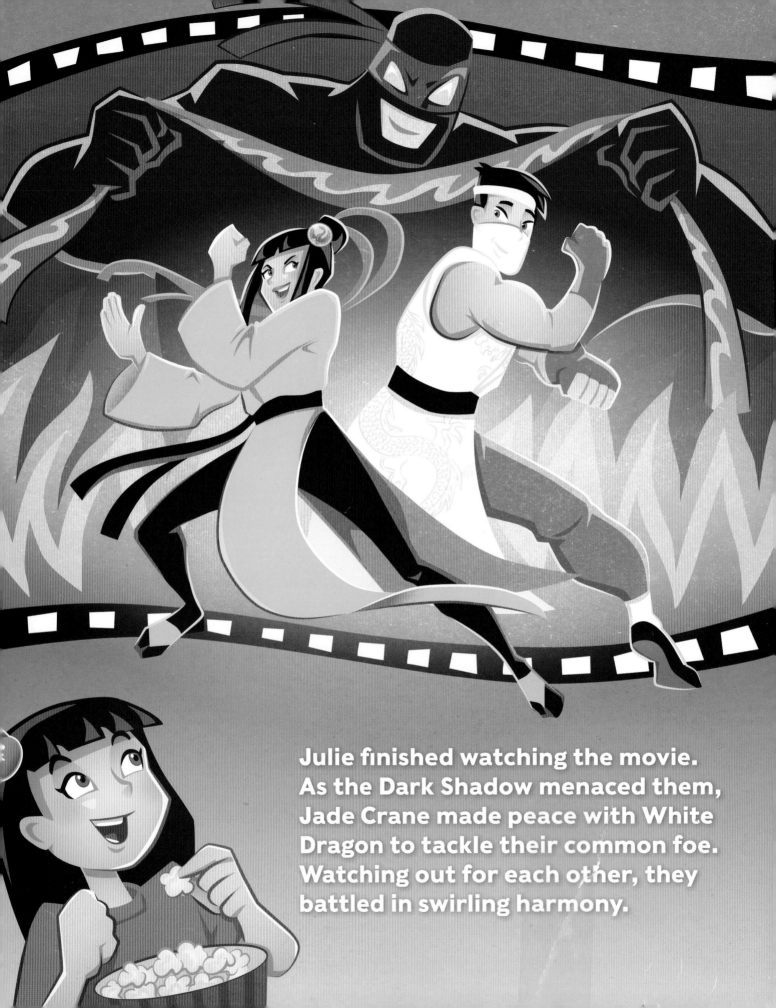

Julie finished watching the movie. As the Dark Shadow menaced them, Jade Crane made peace with White Dragon to tackle their common foe. Watching out for each other, they battled in swirling harmony.

After their thrilling victory,
their Master approached them.

"Congratulations!" she
announced. "I will guard
the Belt of Fire, but give you
these tokens to honor your
achievement and friendship."

Wow!
They did it!

Finally it was time for their orange belt test! At school, Mom, Dad, and Johnny met Brandon's parents.

On the floor Julie and Brandon stood side by side, waiting for Sifu's signal. "Begin!"

"Let's go!" nodded Brandon.

Julie and Brandon sprung from stances into fast sweeps. Pounding the floor, they traded places on offense and defense.

The pair sparred no longer as adversaries but as allies. Sifu approved. "Very good!" he smiled.

When the exam was done, Dad hugged Julie,
"Tiger, you look great in orange!"

Mom remarked,
"But it's too bad
that Master Zhou is
going back home today."

"Yes, but before she leaves, Master Zhou has some presents for Julie and Brandon," mentioned Sifu.

The wise woman grinned, "Your Sifu is lucky to have students like you."

Then Mr. Fong escorted her outside.

Julie opened her box and discovered a familiar-looking piece of jewelry.

"Hey, wait a minute!" laughed Julie in disbelief. Holding her new belt and gift, she ran toward the door and into the sunlight beyond.

THE BELT OF FIRE

To Julie,
Keep flying high!

~ Master Zhou